The Very NOISY Night

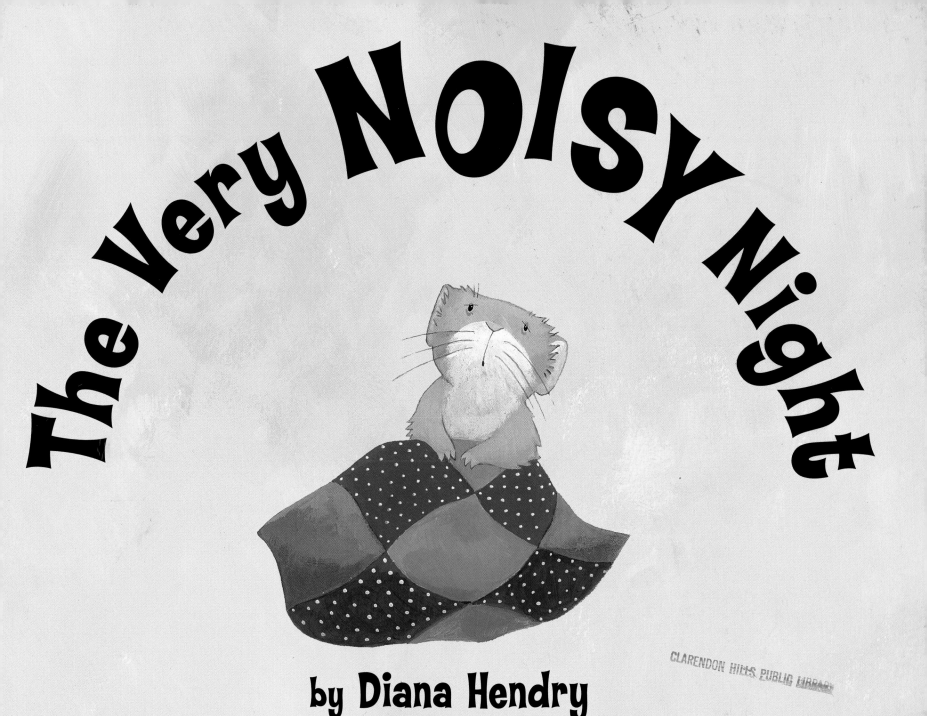

by Diana Hendry

illustrated by Jane Chapman

Dutton Children's Books · New York

It was the middle of the night, and Big Mouse was fast asleep in his big bed. Little Mouse was wide awake in his little bed.

"Big Mouse! Big Mouse!" called Little Mouse. "I can hear something rushing around the house, huffing and puffing."

Big Mouse opened one eye and lifted
one ear. "It's only the wind," he said.

"Can I come into your bed?"
asked Little Mouse.

"No," said Big Mouse. "There isn't room." And
he turned over and went back to sleep.

Little Mouse lay listening
to the wind. Then suddenly,
between a huff and a puff,
came a . . .

TAP

TAP

TAP

TAP

Little Mouse climbed out of bed, opened
the front door—just a crack—and peeped out.

WHOOOSH!

went the wind, but there was no one outside.

"Big Mouse! Big Mouse!" called Little Mouse. "I can hear someone tapping. I think there's a burglar on the roof."

Big Mouse got out of
bed and opened the bedroom
curtains. "Look," he said. "It's only
a branch tapping on the window.
Go back to sleep."

"Can I come into your bed?"
asked Little Mouse.

"No," said Big Mouse. "You
wriggle."

Little Mouse lay in his own bed and listened to the wind huffing and puffing and the branch tap-tapping—and someone calling,

"HOO-HOO!

HOO-HOO!"

Little Mouse climbed out of bed again. This time he looked under it. Then he looked in the wardrobe, and feeling very frightened, he yelled, "Big Mouse! Big Mouse! I think there's a ghost in the room, and it's looking for someone. It keeps calling, 'Who-who, who-who!'"

Big Mouse sighed, sat up, and listened. "It's only an owl," he said. "It stays up all night, like you."

"Can I come into your bed?" asked Little Mouse.

"No," said Big Mouse. "Your paws are always cold." Big Mouse pulled the blanket over his head and went back to sleep, and Little Mouse got back into his own bed.

Little Mouse sat up and
listened to the wind
huffing and puffing,
and the branch
tap-tapping, and
the owl hooting.
But *shhh!*
What was that?

"Big Mouse! Big Mouse!" he called.
"I think it's raining inside." And Little Mouse jumped
out of bed and fetched his red umbrella.

Big Mouse got out of bed, too. He opened the front door to see if it was raining at all. Then Big Mouse went into the kitchen and turned off the dripping faucet. He gently pried the umbrella out of Little Mouse's paws and put it away.

"Can I come into your bed?"
asked Little Mouse.

"No, you're nice and snug in your own bed," said
Big Mouse, taking him back to the bedroom.

Little Mouse lay and listened
to the wind huffing and puffing,
the branch tap-tapping, and the
owl hooting. And just as he was
beginning to feel very sleepy
indeed, he heard . . .

"**WHEEE,**
WHEEE,
WHEEEEE!"

"Big Mouse! Big Mouse!"
he called. "You're snoring."

Wearily, Big Mouse got up. He put his earmuffs on Little Mouse's ears. He put a paper clip on his own nose, and he went back to bed.

Little Mouse lay and listened to—nothing!
It was very, very, very quiet. He couldn't hear
the wind huffing or the branch tapping or the owl
hooting or Big Mouse snoring. It was so quiet that
Little Mouse felt he was all alone in the world.

He took off the earmuffs. He got out of bed
and pulled the paper clip off Big Mouse's nose.
"Big Mouse! Big Mouse!" he cried. "I'm lonely!"

Big Mouse flung back his blanket. "Better come into my bed," he said. So Little Mouse hopped in, and his paws were cold . . .

and he needed just a little wriggle before he fell fast asleep.

Big Mouse lay and listened to the wind huffing and puffing and the branch tap-tapping and the owl hooting and Little Mouse snuffling, and very soon he heard the birds waking up. But neither of them heard the alarm clock . . .

BECAUSE THEY WERE
BOTH FAST ASLEEP!

For Emelia
—D.H.

For Anthony, Jane, Mark,
Katy, and Alice, with love
—J.C.

Published in the United States 1999 by Dutton Children's Books, a division of Penguin Putnam Books for Young Readers
345 Hudson Street, New York, New York 10014 · http://www.penguinputnam.com/yreaders/index.htm

Originally published in the United Kingdom 1999 by Little Tiger Press, London
Typography by Alan Carr · Printed in Singapore · First American Edition · ISBN 0-525-46261-9
2 4 6 8 10 9 7 5 3 1